The adventures of Otto

Going Somewhere

David Milgrim

Ready-to-Read

Simon Spotlight

New York   London   Toronto   Sydney   New Delhi

For my mother with love

SIMON SPOTLIGHT
An imprint of Simon & Schuster Children's Publishing Division
1230 Avenue of the Americas, New York, New York 10020
This Simon Spotlight edition December 2021
Copyright © 2021 by David Milgrim
All rights reserved, including the right of reproduction in whole
or in part in any form.
SIMON SPOTLIGHT, READY-TO-READ, and colophon are registered
trademarks of Simon & Schuster, Inc.
For information about special discounts for bulk purchases,
please contact Simon & Schuster Special Sales at 1-866-506-1949 or
business@simonandschuster.com.
Manufactured in the United States of America 1121 LAK
2 4 6 8 10 9 7 5 3 1
This book has been cataloged with the Library of Congress.
ISBN 978-1-5344-8931-8 (hc)
ISBN 978-1-5344-8930-1 (pbk)
ISBN 978-1-5344-8932-5 (eBook)

See Otto.

See Otto go.

See Pip.

See Pip go too.

"Where are we going?" asks Pip.

"Nowhere," says Otto.

"Oh," says Pip.

"No," says Otto.

"Not yet."

"I see," says Pip.

"How about now?"
says Pip.

"Nope," says Otto.

"Now?" asks Pip.
"No, sir," says Otto.

"Is this nowhere?"
asks Pip.
"Not at all," says Otto.

"I did not think so," says Pip.

"Hey! We are back home where we started," says Pip.

"See?" says Otto.

"Oh," says Pip.

"Can we go
there again?"